The Listener

Algernon Blackwood

The Listener

Table of Contents

The Listener..1
    Algernon Blackwood..1

The Listener

Algernon Blackwood

Kessinger Publishing reprints thousands of hard-to-find books!

Visit us at http://www.kessinger.net

Sept. 4.—I have hunted all over London for rooms suited to my income—£120 a year—and have at last found them. Two rooms, without modern conveniences, it is true, and in an old, ramshackle building, but within a stone's throw of P— Place and in an eminently respectable street. The rent is only £ 25 a year. I had begun to despair when at last I found them by chance.

The chance was a mere chance, and unworthy of record. I had to sign a lease for a year, and I did so willingly. The furniture from our old place in Hampshire, which has been stored so long, will just suit them.

Oct. 1.—Here I am in my two rooms, in the centre of London, and not far from the offices of the periodicals, where occasionally I dispose of an article or two. The building is at the end of a cul-de-sac. The alley is well paved and clean, and lined chiefly with the backs of sedate and institutional-looking buildings. There is a stable in it. My own house is dignified with the title of "Chambers ". I feel as if one day the honour must prove too much for it, and it will swell with pride—and fall asunder. It is very old. The floor of my sitting-room has valleys and low hills on it, and the top of the door slants away from the ceiling with a glorious disregard of what is usual.

They must have quarrelled—fifty years ago—and have been going apart ever since.

The Listener

Oct. 2.—My landlady is old and thin, with a faded, dusty face. She is uncommunicative. The few words she utters seem to cost her pain. Probably her lungs are half choked with dust. She keeps my rooms as free from this commodity as possible, and has the assistance of a strong girl who brings up the breakfast and lights the fire. As I have said already, she is not communicative.

In reply to pleasant efforts on my part she informed me briefly that I was the only occupant of the house at present. My rooms had not been occupied for some years. There had been other gen–tlemen upstairs, but they had left.

She never looks straight at me when she speaks, but fixes her dim eyes on my middle waistcoat button, till I get nervous and begin to think it isn't on straight, or is the wrong sort of button altogether.

Oct. 8.—My week's book is nicely kept, and so far is reasonable. Milk and sugar 7d., bread 6d., butter 8d., marmalade 6d., eggs 1s. 8d., laundress 2s. 9d., oil 6d., attendance 5s.; total 12s. 2d.

The landlady has a son who, she told me, is "somethink on a homnibus". He comes occasionally to see her. I think he drinks, for he talks very loud, regardless of the hour of the day or night, and tumbles about over the furniture downstairs.

All the morning I sit indoors writing—articles; verses for the comic papers; a novel I've been "at" for three years, and concerning which I have dreams; a children's book, in which the imagination has free rein; and another book which is to last as long as myself, since it is an honest record of my soul's advance or retreat in the struggle of life. Besides these, I keep a book of poems which I use as a safety valve, and concerning which I have no dreams whatsoever.

Between the lot I am always occupied. In the afternoons I generally try to take a walk for my health's sake, through Regent's Park, into Kensington Gardens, or farther afield to Hampstead.Heath.

Oct. 10.—Everything went wrong to-day. I have two eggs for breakfast. This morning one of them was bad. I rang the bell for Emily. When she came in I was reading the paper, and, without looking up, I said, "Egg's bad." "Oh, is it, sir? " she said; "I'll get

The Listener

another one," and went out, taking the egg with her. I waited my breakfast for her return, which was in five minutes. She put the new egg on the table and went away. But, when I looked down, I saw that she had taken away the good egg and left the bad one—all green and yellow—in the slop basin. I rang again.

"You've taken the wrong egg," I said.

"Oh! " she exclaimed; " I thought the one I took down didn't smell so very bad." In due time she returned with the good egg, and I resumed my breakfast with two eggs, but less appetite. It was all very trivial, to be sure, but so stupid that I felt annoyed. The character of that egg influ-enced everything I did. I wrote a bad article, and tore it up. I got a bad headache. I used bad words—to myself. Everything was bad, so I "chucked" work and went for a long walk.

I dined at a cheap chop-house on my way back, and reached home about nine o'clock.

Rain was just beginning to fall as I came in, and the wind was rising. It promised an ugly night. The alley looked dismal and dreary, and the hall of the house, as I passed through it, felt chilly as a tomb. It was the first stormy night I had experienced in my new quarters. The draughts were awful. They came criss-cross, met in the middle of the room, and formed eddies and whirlpools and cold silent currents that almost lifted the hair of my head. I stuffed up the sashes of the windows with neckties and odd socks, and sat over the smoky fire to keep warm. First I tried to write, but found it too cold. My hand turned to ice on the paper.

What tricks the wind did play with the old place! It came rushing up the forsaken alley with a sound like the feet of a hurrying crowd of people who stopped suddenly at the door. I felt as if a lot of curious folk had arranged themselves just outside and were staring up at my windows.

Then they took to their heels again and fled whispering and laughing down the lane, only, however, to return with the next gust of wind and repeat their impertinence. On the other side of my room a single square window opens into a sort of shaft, or well, that measures about six feet across to the back wall of another house. Down this funnel the wind dropped, and puffed and shouted. Such noises I never heard before. Between these two entertainments I sat over the fire in a great-coat, listening to the deep booming in the

The Listener

chimney. It was like being in a ship at sea, and I almost looked for the floor to rise in undulations and rock to and fro.

Oct. 12.—I wish I were not quite so lonely—and so poor. And yet I love both my loneliness and my poverty. The former makes me appreciate the companionship of the wind and rain, while the latter preserves my liver and prevents me wasting time in dancing attendance upon women.

Poor, ill-dressed men are not acceptable "attendants".

My parents are dead, and my only sister is—no, not dead exactly, but married to a very rich man. They travel most of the time, he to find his health, she to lose herself. Through sheer neglect on her part she has long passed out of my life. The door closed when, after an absolute silence of five years, she sent me a cheque for £50 at Christmas. It was signed by her husband! I returned it to her in a thousand pieces and in an unstamped envelope. So at least I had the satisfaction of knowing that it cost her something! She wrote back with a broad quill pen that covered a whole page with three lines, "You are evidently as cracked as ever, and rude and ungrateful into the bargain." It had always been my special terror lest the insanity of my father's family should leap across the generations and appear in me. This thought haunted me, and she.knew it. So after this little exchange of civilities the door slammed, never to open again. I heard the crash it made, and, with it, the falling from the walls of my heart of many little bits of china with their own peculiar value—rare china, some of it, that only needed dusting. The same walls, too, carried mirrors in which I used sometimes to see reflected the misty lawns of childhood, the daisy chains, the wind-torn blossoms scattered through the orchard by warm rains, the robbers'
cave in the long walk, and the hidden store of apples in the hayloft. She was my inseparable companion then—but, when the door slammed, the mirrors cracked across their entire length, and the visions they held vanished for ever. Now I am quite alone. At forty one cannot begin all over again to build up careful friendships, and all others are comparatively worthless.

Oct. 14.—My bedroom is 10 by 10. It is below the level of the front room, and a step leads down into it. Both rooms are very quiet on calm nights, for there is no traffic down this forsaken alley-way. In spite of the occasional larks of the wind, it is a most sheltered strip. At its upper end, below my windows, all the cats of the neighbourhood congregate as soon as darkness gathers. They lie undisturbed on the long ledge of a blind window of

The Listener

the opposite building, for after the postman has come and gone at 9.30, no footsteps ever dare to interrupt their sinister conclave, no step but my own, or sometimes the unsteady footfall of the son who "is somethink on a homnibus".

Oct. 15.—I dined at an "A.B.C." shop on poached eggs and coffee, and then went for a stroll round the outer edge of Regent's Park. It was ten o'clock when I got home. I counted no less than thirteen cats, all of a dark colour, crouching under the lee side of the alley walls. It was a cold night, and the stars shone like points of ice in a blue–black sky. The cats turned their heads and stared at me in silence as I passed. An odd sensation of shyness took possession of me under the glare of so many pairs of unblinking eyes. As I fumbled with the latch–key they jumped noise–lessly down and pressed against my legs, as if anxious to be let in. But I slammed the door in their faces and ran quickly upstairs. The front room, as I entered to grope for the matches, felt as cold as a stone vault, and the air held an unusual dampness.

Oct. 17.—For several days I have been working on a ponderous article that allows no play for the fancy. My imagination requires a judicious rein; I am afraid to let it loose, for it carries me sometimes into appalling places beyond the stars and beneath the world. No one realises the danger more than I do. But what a foolish thins to write here—for there is no one to know, no one to realize! My mind of late has held unusual thoughts, thoughts I have never had before, about medicines and drugs and the treatment of strange illnesses. I cannot imagine their source.

At no time in my life have I dwelt upon such ideas now constantly throng my brain. I have had no exercise lately, for the weather has been shocking; and all my afternoons have been spent in the reading–room of the British Museum, where I have a reader's ticket.

I have made an unpleasant discovery: there are rats in the house. At night from my bed I have heard them scampering across the hills and valleys of the front room, and my sleep has been a good deal disturbed in consequence.

Oct. 19.—The landlady, I find, has a little boy with her, probably her son's child. In fine weather he plays in the alley, and draws a wooden cart over the cobbles. One of the wheels is off, and it makes a most distracting noise. After putting up with it as long as possible, I found it was getting on my nerves, and I could not write. So I rang the bell.

The Listener

Emily answered it.

"Emily, will you ask the little fellow to make less noise? It's impossible to work."

The girl went downstairs, and soon afterwards the child was called in by the kitchen door. I felt rather a brute for spoiling his play. In a few minutes, however, the noise began again, and I felt that he was the brute. He dragged the broken toy with a string over the stones till the rattling noise jarred every nerve in my body. It became unbearable, and I rang the bell a second time.

"That noise must be put a stop to!" I said to the girl, with decision.

"Yes, sir," she grinned, "I know; but one of the wheels is hoff. The men in the stable offered to mend it for 'im, but he wouldn't let them. He says he likes it that way."

"I can't help what he likes. The noise must stop. I can't write."

"Yes, sir; I'll tell Mrs. Monson."

The noise stopped for the day then.

Oct. 23.—Every day for the past week that cart has rattled over the stones, till I have come to think of it as a huge carrier's van with four wheels and two horses; and every morning I have been obliged to ring the bell and have it stopped. The last time Mrs. Monson herself came up, and said she was sorry I had been annoyed; the sounds should not occur again. With rare discursiveness she went on to ask if I was comfortable, and how I liked the rooms. I replied cautiously. I mentioned the rats. She said they were mice. I spoke of the draughts. She said, "Yes, it were a draughty 'ouse." I referred to the cats, and she said they had been as long as she could remember. By way of conclusion, she informed me that the house was over two hundred years old, and that the last gentleman who had occupied my rooms was a painter who "'ad real Jimmy Bueys and Raffles 'anging all hover the walls". It took me some moments to discern that Cimabue and Raphael were in the woman's mind.

Oct. 24.—Last night the son who is "somethink on a homnibus" came in. He had evidently been drinking, for I heard loud and angry voices below in the kitchen long after

The Listener

I had gone to bed. Once, too, I caught the singular words rising up to me through the floor, "Burning from top to bottom is the only thing that'll ever make this 'ouse right." I knocked on the floor, and the voices ceased suddenly, though later I again heard their clamour in my dreams.

These rooms are very quiet, almost too quiet sometimes. On windless nights they are silent as the grave, and the house might be miles in the country. The roar of London's traffic reaches me only in heavy, distant vibrations. It holds an ominous note sometimes, like that of an approaching army, or an immense tidal-wave very far away thundering in the night.

Oct. 27.—Mrs. Monson, though admirably silent, is a foolish, fussy woman. She does such stupid things. In dusting the room she puts all my things in the wrong places. The ash-trays, which should be on the writing-table, she sets in a silly row on the mantelpiece. The pen-tray, which should be beside the inkstand, she hides away cleverly among the books on my reading-desk.

My gloves she arranges daily in idiotic array upon a half-filled bookshelf, and I always have to rearrange them on the low table by the door. She places my armchair at impossible angles between the fire and the light, and the tablecloth—the one with Trinity Hall stains—she puts on the table in such a fashion that when I look at it I feel as if my tie and all my clothes were on crooked and awry. She exasperates me. Her very silence and meekness are irritating.

Sometimes I feel inclined to throw the inkstand at her, just to bring an expression into her watery eyes and a squeak from those colourless lips. Dear me! What violent expressions I am making use of! How very foolish of me! And yet it almost seems as if the words were not my own, but.had been spoken into my ear—I mean, I never make use of such terms naturally.

Oct. 30.—I have been here a month. The place does not agree with me, I think. My headaches are more frequent and violent, and my nerves are a perpetual source of discomfort and annoyance.

I have conceived a great dislike for Mrs. Monson, a feeling I am certain she reciprocates.

The Listener

Somehow, the impression comes frequently to me that there are goings on in this house of which I know nothing, and which she is careful to hide from me.

Last night her son slept in the house, and this morning as I was standing at the window I saw him go out. He glanced up and caught my eye. It was a loutish figure and a singularly repulsive face that I saw, and he gave me the benefit of a very unpleasant leer. At least, so I imagined.

Evidently I am getting absurdly sensitive to trifles, and I suppose it is my disordered nerves making themselves felt. In the British Museum this afternoon I noticed several people at the readers' table staring at me and watching every movement I made. Whenever I looked up from my books I found their eyes upon me. It seemed to me unnecessary and unpleasant, and I left earlier than was my custom. When I reached the door I threw back a last look into the room, and saw every head at the table turned in my direction. It annoyed me very much, and yet I know it is foolish to take note of such things. When I am well they pass me by. I must get more regular exercise. Of late I have had next to none.

Nov. 2.—The utter stillness of this house is beginning to oppress me. I wish there were other fellows living upstairs. No footsteps ever sound overhead, and no tread ever passes my door to go up the next flight of stairs. I am beginning to feel some curiosity to go up myself and see what the upper rooms are like. I feel lonely here and isolated, swept into a deserted corner of the world and forgotten. . . . Once I actually caught myself gazing into the long, cracked mirrors, trying to sec the sunlight dancing beneath the trees in the orchard. But only deep shadows seemed to congregate there now, and I soon desisted.

It has been very dark all day, and no wind stirring. The fogs have begun. I had to use a reading–lamp all this morning. There was no cart to be heard to–day. I actually missed it. This morning, in the gloom and silence, I think I could almost have welcomed it. After all, the sound is a very human one, and this empty house at the end of the alley holds other noises that are not quite so satisfactory.

I have never once seen a policeman in the lane, and the postmen always hurry out with no evidence of a desire to loiter.

The Listener

10 p.m.—As I write this I hear no sound but the deep murmur of the distant traffic and the low sighing of the wind. The two sounds melt into one another. Now and again a cat raises its shrill, uncanny cry upon the darkness. The cats are always there under my windows when the darkness falls. The wind is dropping into the funnel with a noise like the sudden sweeping of immense distant wings. It is a dreary night. I feel lost and forgotten.

Nov. 3—From my windows I can see arrivals. When anyone comes to the door I can just see the hat and shoulders and the hand on the bell. Only two fellows have been to see me since I came here two months ago. Both of them I saw from the window before they came tip, and heard their voices asking if I was in. Neither of them ever came back.

I have finished the ponderous article. On reading it through, however, I was dissatisfied with it, and drew my pencil through almost every page. There were strange expressions and ideas in it.that 1 could not explain, and viewed with amazement, not to say alarm. They did not sound like my very own, and I could not remember having written them. Can it be that my memory is beginning to be affected?p

My pens are never to be found. That stupid old woman puts them in a different place each day. I must give her due credit for finding so many new hiding places; such ingenuity is wonderful. I have told her repeatedly, but she always says, "I'll speak to Emily, sir." Emily always says, "I'll tell Mrs. Monson, sir." Their foolishness makes me irritable and scatters all my thoughts. I should like to stick the lost pens into them and turn them out, blind-eyed, to be scratched and mauled by those thousand hungry cats. Whew! What a ghastly thought! Where in the world did it come from? Such an idea is no more my own than it is the policeman's. Yet I felt I had to write it. It was like a voice singing in my head, and my pen wouldn't stop till the last word was finished. What ridiculous nonsense! I must and will restrain myself. 1 must take more regular exercise; my nerves and liver plague me horribly.

Nov. 4.—I attended a curious lecture in the French quarter on "Death", but the room was so hot and I was so weary that I fell asleep. The only part I heard, however, touched my imagination vividly. Speaking of suicides, the lecturer said that self-murder was no escape from the miseries of the present, but only a preparation of greater sorrow for the future. Suicides, he declared, cannot shirk their responsibilities so easily. They must return to take up life exactly where they laid it so violently down, but with the added pain

The Listener

and punishment of their weakness. Many of them wander the earth in unspeakable misery till they can reclothe themselves in the body of someone else—generally a lunatic, or weak-minded person, who cannot resist the hideous obsession. This is their only means of escape. Surely a weird and horrible idea! I wish I had slept all the time and not heard it at all. My mind is morbid enough without such ghastly fancies. Such mischievous propaganda should be stopped by the police. I'll write to the Times and suggest it.

Good idea!

I walked home through Greek Street, Soho, and imagined that a hundred years had slipped back into place and De Quincey was still there, haunting the night with invocations to his "just, subtle, and mighty" drug. His vast dreams seemed to hover not very far away. Once started in my brain, the pictures refused to go away; and I saw him sleeping in that cold, tenantless mansion with the strange little waif who was afraid of its ghosts, both together in the shadows under a single horseman's cloak; or wandering in the companionship of the spectral Anne; or, later still, on his way to the eternal rendezvous at the foot of Great Titchfield Street, the rendezvous she never was able to keep. What an unutterable gloom, what an untold horror of sorrow and suffering comes over me as I try to realise something of what that man—boy he then was—must have taken into his lonely heart.

As I came up the alley I saw a light in the top window, and a head and shoulders thrown in an exaggerated shadow upon the blind. I wondered what the son could be doing up there at such an hour.

Nov. 5.—This morning, while writing, someone came up the creaking stairs and knocked cautiously at my door. Thinking it was the landlady, I said, "Come in!" The knock was repeated, and I cried louder, "Come in, come in!" But no one turned the handle, and I continued my writing with a vexed "Well, stay out, then!" under my breath. Went on writing? I tried to, but my thoughts had suddenly dried up at their source. I could not set down a single word. It was a dark, yellow-fog morning, and there was little enough inspiration in the air as it was, but that stupid.woman standing just outside my door waiting to be told again to come in roused a spirit of vexation that filled my head to the exclusion of all else. At last I jumped up and opened the door myself.

The Listener

"What do you want, and why in the world don't you come in?" I cried out. But the words dropped into empty air. There was no one there. The fog poured up the dingy staircase in deep yellow coils, but there was no sign of a human being anywhere.

I slammed the door, with imprecations upon the house and its noises, and went back to my work. A few minutes later Emily came in with a letter.

"Were you or Mrs. Monson outside a few minutes ago knocking at my door?"

"No, sir."

"Are you sure?p

"Mrs. Monson's gone to market, and there's no one but me and the child in the 'ole 'ouse, and I've been washing the dishes for the last hour, sir."

I fancied the girl's face turned a shade paler. She fidgeted towards the door with a glance over her shoulder.

"Wait, Emily," I said, and then told her what I had heard. She stared stupidly at me, though her eyes shifted now and then over the articles in the room.

"Who was it? "I asked when I had come to the end. "Mrs. Monson says it's honly mice," she said, as if repeating a learned lesson.

"Mice!" I exclaimed; "it's nothing of the sort. Someone was feeling about outside my door.

Who was it? Is the son in the house?"

Her whole manner changed suddenly, and she became earnest instead of evasive. She seemed anxious to tell the truth.

"Oh no, sir; there's no one in the house at all but you and me and the child, and there couldn't 'ave been nobody at your door. As for them knocks—" She stopped abruptly, as though she had said too much.

The Listener

"Well, what about the knocks?" I said more gently.

"Of course," she stammered, "the knocks isn't mice, nor the footsteps neither, but then—"

Again she came to a full halt.

"Anything wrong with the house?"

"Lor', no, sir; the drains is splendid!"

"I don't mean drains, girl. I mean, did anything—anything bad ever happen here?"

She flushed up to the roots of her hair, and then turned suddenly pale again. She was obviously in considerable distress, and there was something she was anxious, yet afraid to tell— some forbidden thing she was not allowed to mention.

"I don't mind what it was, only I should like to know," I said encouragingly.

Raising her frightened eyes to my face, she began to blurt out something about "that which 'appened once to a gentleman that lived hupstairs", when a shrill voice calling her name sounded below.

"Emily, Emily!" It was the returning landlady, and the girl tumbled downstairs as if pulled backwards by a rope, leaving me full of conjectures as to what in the world could have happened to a gentleman upstairs that could in so curious a manner affect my ears downstairs.

Nov. 10.—I have done capital work; have finished the ponderous article and had it accepted for the Review, and another one ordered. I feel well and cheerful, and have had regular exercise and good sleep; no headaches, no nerves, no liver! Those pills the chemist recommended are.wonderful. I can watch the child playing with his cart and feel no annoyance; sometimes I almost feel inclined to join him. Even the grey-faced landlady rouses pity in me; I am sorry for her: so worn, so weary, so oddly put together, just like the building. She looks as if she had once suffered some shock of terror, and was momentarily dreading another. When I spoke to her to-day very gently about not putting the pens in the ash-tray and the gloves on the hook-shelf she raised her faint eyes to mine for the first time, and said with the ghost of a smile, "I'll try and re-member, sir." I felt inclined to pat her on the back and say, "Come, cheer up and be jolly. Life's not so bad after all." Oh! I am much better. There's nothing like open air and success and good sleep. They build up as if by magic the portions of the heart eaten down by despair and unsatisfied yearnings. Even to the cats I feel friendly. When I came in at eleven o'clock to-night they followed me to the door in a stream, and I stooped down to stroke the one nearest to me.

Bah! The brute hissed and spat, and struck at me with her paws. The claw caught my hand and drew blood in a thin line. The others danced sideways into the darkness, screeching, as though I had done them an injury. I believe these cats really hate me. Perhaps they are only waiting to be reinforced. Then they will attack me. Ha, ha! In spite of the momentary annoyance, this fancy sent me laughing upstairs to my room.

The fire was out, and the room seemed unusually cold. As I groped my way over to the mantelpiece to find the matches I realised all at once that there was another person standing beside me in the darkness. I could, of course, see nothing, but my fingers, feeling along the ledge, came into forcible contact with something that was at once withdrawn. It was cold and moist. I could have sworn it was somebody's hand. My flesh began to creep instantly.

"Who's that?" I exclaimed in a loud voice.

My voice dropped into the silence like a pebble into a deep well. There was no answer, but at the same moment I heard someone moving away from me across the room in the direction of the door. It was a confused sort of footstep, and the sound of garments brushing the furniture on the way. The same second my hand stumbled upon the match-box, and I struck a light. I expected to see Mrs. Monson, or Emily, or perhaps the son who is something on an omnibus. But the flare of the gas-jet illumined an empty room; there was not a sign of a person anywhere. I felt the hair stir upon my head, and instinctively I backed tip against the wall, lest something should approach me from behind. I was distinctly alarmed. But the next minute I recovered myself. The door was open on to the landing, and I crossed the room, not without some inward trepidation, and went out. The light from the room fell upon the stairs, but there was no one to be seen anywhere, nor was there any sound on the creaking wooden staircase to indicate a departing creature.

The Listener

I was in the act of turning to go in again when a sound overhead caught my ear. It was a very faint sound, not unlike the sigh of wind; yet it could not have been the wind, for the night was still as the grave. Though it was not repeated, I resolved to go upstairs and see for myself what it all meant. Two senses had been affected—touch and hearing—and I could not believe that I had been deceived. So, with a lighted candle, I went stealthily forth on my unpleasant journey into the upper regions of this queer little old house.

On the first landing there was only one door, and it was locked. On the second there was also only one door, but when I turned the handle it opened. There came forth to meet me the chill musty air that is characteristic of a long unoccupied room. With it there came an indescribable odour. I use the adjective advisedly. Though very faint, diluted as it were, it was nevertheless an odour that made my gorge rise. I had never smelt anything like it before, and I cannot describe it.

The room was small and square, close under the roof, with a sloping ceiling and two tiny windows. It was cold as the grave, without a shred of carpet or a stick of furniture. The icy.atmosphere and the nameless odour combined to make the room abominable to me, and, after lingering a moment to see that it contained no cupboards or corners into which a person might have crept for concealment, I made haste to shut the door, and went downstairs again to bed.

Evidently I had been deceived after all as to the noise.

In the night I had a foolish but very vivid dream. I dreamed that the landlady and another person, dark and not properly visible, entered my room on all fours, followed by a horde of immense cats. They attacked me as I lay in bed, and murdered me, and then dragged my body upstairs and deposited it on the floor of that cold little square room under the roof.

Nov. 11.—Since my talk with Emily—the unfinished talk—I have hardly once set eyes on her. Mrs. Monson now attends wholly to my wants. As usual, she does everything exactly as I don't like it done. It is all too utterly trivial to mention, but it is exceedingly irritating. Like small doses of morphine often repeated, she has finally a cumulative effect.

The Listener

Nov. 12.—This morning I woke early, and came into the front room to get a book, meaning to read in bed till it was time to get tip. Emily was laying the fire.

"Good morning!" I said cheerfully. "Mind you make a good fire. It's very cold."

The girl turned and showed me a startled face. It was not Emily at all!

"Where's Emily? " I exclaimed.

"You mean the girl as was 'ere before me?"

"Has Emily left?"

"I came on the 6th," she replied sullenly, "and she'd gone then." I got my book and went back to bed. Emily must have been sent away almost immediately after our conversation. This reflection kept coming between me and the printed page. I was glad when it was time to get up.

Such prompt energy, such merciless decision, seemed to argue something of importance—to somebody.

Nov. 13.—The wound inflicted by the cat's claw has swollen, and causes me annoyance and some pain. It throbs and itches. I'm afraid my blood must be in poor condition, or it would have healed by now. I opened it with a penknife soaked in an antiseptic solution, and cleansed it thoroughly. I have heard unpleasant stories of the results of wounds inflicted by cats.

Nov. 14.—In spite of the curious effect this house certainly exercises upon my nerves, I like it. It is lonely and deserted in the very heart of London, but it is also for that reason quiet to work in. I wonder why it is so cheap. Some people might he suspicious, but I did not even ask the reason. No answer is better than a lie. If only I could remove the cats from the outside and the rats from the inside. I feel that I shall grow accustomed more and more to its peculiarities, and shall die here. Ah, that expression reads queerly and gives a wrong impression: I meant live and die here. I shall renew the lease from year to year till one of us crumbles to pieces. From present indications the building will be the first to go.

The Listener

Nov. 16.—It is abominable the way my nerves go up and down with me—and rather discouraging. This morning I woke to find my clothes scattered about the room, and a cane chair overturned beside the bed. My coat and waistcoat looked just as if they had been tried on by someone in the night. I had horribly vivid dreams, too, in which someone covering his face with his hands kept coming close up to me, crying out as if in pain. "Where can I find covering? Oh,.who will clothe me?" How silly, and yet it frightened me a little. It was so dreadfully real. It is now over a year since I last walked in my sleep and woke up with such a shock on the cold pavement of Earl's Court Road, where I then lived. I thought I was cured, but evidently not. This discovery has rather a disquieting effect upon me. To-night I shall resort to the old trick of tying my toe to the bed-post.

Nov. 17.—Last night I was again troubled by most oppressive dreams. Someone seemed to be moving in the night up and down my room, sometimes passing into the front room, and then returning to stand beside the bed and stare intently down upon me. I was being watched by this person all night long. I never actually awoke, though I was often very near it. I suppose it was a nightmare from indigestion, for this morning I have one of my old vile headaches. Yet all my clothes lay about the floor when I awoke, where they had evidently been flung (had I so tossed them?) during the dark hours, and my trousers trailed over the step into the front room.

Worse than this, though—I fancied I noticed about the room in the morning that strange, fetid odour. Though very faint, its mere suggestion is foul and nauseating. 'What in the world can it be, I wonder? . . . In future I shall lock my door.

Nov. 26.—I have accomplished a lot of good work during this past week, and have also managed to get regular exercise. I have felt well and in an equable state of mind. Only two things have occurred to disturb my equanimity. The first is trivial in itself, and no doubt to be easily explained. The upper window where I saw the light on the night of November 4, with the shadow of a large head and shoulders upon the blind, is one of the windows in the square room under the roof. In reality it has no blind at all!

Here is the other thing. I was coming home last night in a fresh fall of snow about eleven o'clock, my umbrella low down over my head. Half-way up the alley, where the snow was wholly untrodden, I saw a man's legs in front of me. The umbrella hid the rest of his figure, but on raising it I saw that he was tall and broad and was walking, as I was,

The Listener

towards the door of my house. He could not have been four feet ahead of me. I had thought the alley was empty when I entered it, but might of course have been mistaken very easily.

A sudden gust of wind compelled me to lower the umbrella, and when I raised it again, not half a minute later, there was no longer any man to be seen. With a few more steps I reached the door. It was closed as usual. I then noticed with a sudden sensation of dismay that the surface of the freshly fallen snow was unbroken. My own foot-marks were the only ones to be seen anywhere, and though I retraced my way to tile point where I had first seen the man, I could find no slightest impression of any other boots. Feeling creepy and uncomfortable, I went upstairs, and was glad to get into bed.

Nov. 28.—With the fastening of my bedroom door the disturbances ceased. I am convinced that I walked in my sleep. Probably I untied my toe and then tied it up again. The fancied security of the locked door would alone have been enough to restore sleep to my troubled spirit and enable me to rest quietly.

Last night, however, the annoyance was suddenly renewed another and more aggressive form. I woke in the darkness with the impression that someone was standing outside my bedroom door listening. As I became more awake the impression grew into positive knowledge.

Though there was no appreciable sound of moving or breathing, I was so convinced of the propinquity of a listener that I crept out of bed and approached the door. As I did so there came.faintly from the next room the unmistakable sound of someone retreating stealthily across the floor. Yet, as I heard it, it was neither the tread of a man nor a regular footstep, but rather, it seemed to me, a confused sort of crawling, almost as of someone on his hands and knees.

I unlocked the door in less than a second, and passed quickly into the front room, and I could feel, as by the subtlest imaginable vibrations upon my nerves, that the spot I was standing in had just that instant been vacated! The Listener had moved; he was now behind the other door, standing in the passage. Yet this door was also closed. I moved swiftly, and as silently as possible, across the floor, and turned the handle. A cold rush of air met me from the passage and sent shiver after shiver down my back. There was no one in the doorway; there was no one on the little landing; there was no one moving

The Listener

down the staircase. Yet I had been so quick that this midnight Listener could not be very far away, and I felt that if I persevered I should eventually come face to face with him. And the courage that came so opportunely to overcome my nervousness and horror seemed born of the unwelcome conviction that it was somehow necessary for my safety as well as my sanity that I should find this intruder and force his secret from him. For was it not the intent action of his mind upon my own, in concentrated listening, that had awakened me with such a vivid realisation of his presence?p

Advancing across the narrow landing, I peered down into the well of the little house. There was nothing to be seen; no one was moving in the darkness. How cold the oilcloth was to my bare feet.

I cannot say what it was that suddenly drew my eyes upwards. I only know that, without apparent reason, I looked up and saw a person about half-way up the next turn of the stairs, leaning forward over the balustrade and staring straight into my face. It was a man. He appeared to be clinging to the rail rather than standing on the stairs. The gloom made it impossible to see much beyond the general outline, but the head and shoulders were seemingly enormous, and stood sharply silhouetted against the skylight in the roof immediately above. The idea flashed into my brain in a moment that I was looking into the visage of something monstrous. The huge skull, the mane-like hair, the wide-humped shoulders, suggested, in a way I did not pause to analyse, that which was scarcely human; and for some seconds, fascinated by horror, I returned the gaze and stared into the dark, inscrutable countenance above me, without knowing exactly where I was or what I was doing.

Then I realised in quite a new way that I was face to face with the secret midnight Listener, and I steeled myself as best I could for what was about to come.

The source of the rash courage that came to me at this awful moment will ever be to me an inexplicable mystery. Though shivering with fear, and my forehead wet with an unholy dew, I resolved to advance. Twenty questions leaped to my lips: What are you? What do you want?p

Why do you listen and watch? Why do you come into my room? But none of them found articulate utterance.

The Listener

I began forthwith to climb the stairs, and with the first signs of my advance he drew himself back into the shadows and began to move. He retreated as swiftly as I advanced. I heard the sound of his crawling motion a few steps ahead of me, ever maintaining the same distance. When I reached the landing he was half-way up the next flight, and when I was half-way up the next flight he had already arrived at the top landing. I then heard him open the door of the little square room under the roof and go in. Immediately, though the door did not close after him, the sound of his moving entirely ceased.

At this moment I longed for a light, or a stick, or any weapon whatsoever; but I had none of these things, and it was impossible to go back. So I marched steadily up the rest of the stairs, and in less than a minute found myself standing in the gloom face to face with the door through which this creature had just entered.

For a moment I hesitated. The door was about half-way open, and the Listener was standing evidently in his favourite attitude just behind it—listening. To search through that dark room for him seemed hopeless; to enter the same small space where he was seemed horrible. The very idea filled me with loathing, and I almost decided to turn back.

It is strange at such times how trivial things impinge on the consciousness with a shock as of something important and immense. Something—it may have been a beetle or a mouse—scuttled over the bare boards behind me. The door moved a quarter of an inch, closing. My decision came back with a sudden rush, as it were, and thrusting out a foot, I kicked the door so that it swung sharply back to its full extent, and permitted me to walk forward slowly into the aperture of profound blackness beyond. What a queer soft sound my bare feet made on the boards! how the blood sang and buzzed in my head!

I was inside. The darkness closed over me, hiding even the windows. I began to grope my way round the walls in a thorough search; but in order to prevent all possibility of the other's escape, I first of all closed the door.

There we were, we two, shut in together between four walls, within a few feet of one another.

But with what, with whom, was I thus momentarily imprisoned? A new light flashed suddenly over the affair with a swift, illuminating brilliance—and I knew I was a fool, an utter fool! I was wide awake at last, and the horror was evaporating. My cursed nerves

The Listener

again; a dream, a nightmare, and the old result—walking in my sleep. The figure was a dream-figure. Many a time before had the actors in my dreams stood before me for some moments after I was awake. . . .

There was a chance match in my pyjamas' pocket, and I struck it on the wall. The room was utterly empty. It held not even a shadow. I went quickly down to bed, cursing my wretched nerves and my foolish, vivid dreams. But as soon as ever I was asleep again, the same uncouth figure of a man crept back to my bedside, and bending over me with his immense head close to my ear, whispered repeatedly in my dreams, "I want your body; I want its covering. I'm waiting for it, and listening always." Words scarcely less foolish than the dream.

But I wonder what that queer odour was up in the square room. I noticed it again, and stronger than ever before, and it seemed to be also in my bedroom when I woke this morning.

Nov. 29.—Slowly, as moonbeams rise over a misty sea in June, the thought is entering my mind that my nerves and somnambulistic dreams do not adequately account for the influence this house exercises upon me. It holds me as with a fine, invisible net. I cannot escape if I would. It draws me, and it means to keep me.

Nov. 30.—The post this morning brought me a letter from Aden, forwarded from my old rooms in Earl's Court. It was from Chapter, my former Trinity chum, who is on his way home from the East, and asks for my address. I sent it to him at the hotel he mentioned, "to await arrival".

As I have already said, my windows command a view of the alley, and I can see an arrival without difficulty. This morning, while I was busy writing, the sound of footsteps coming up the alley filled me with a sense of vague alarm that I could in no way account for. I went over to the window, and saw a man standing below waiting for the door to be opened. His shoulders were broad, his top-hat glossy, and his overcoat fitted beautifully round the collar. All this I could see, but no more. Presently the door was opened, and the shock to my nerves was unmistakable when.I heard a man's voice ask, "Is Mr. — still here?" mentioning my name. I could not catch the answer, but it could only have been in the affirmative, for the man entered the hall and the door shut to behind him. But I waited in vain for the sound of his steps on the stairs. There was no sound of any kind. It seemed

The Listener

to me so strange that I opened my door and looked out. No one was anywhere to be seen. I walked across the narrow landing, and looked through the window that commands the whole length of the alley. There was no sign of a human being, coming or going.

The lane was deserted. Then I deliberately walked downstairs into the kitchen, and asked the grey-faced landlady if a gentleman had just that minute called for me.

The answer, given with an odd, weary sort of smile, was "No!"

Dec. 1.—I feel genuinely alarmed and uneasy over the state of my nerves. Dreams are dreams, but never before have I had dreams in broad daylight.

I am looking forward very much to Chapter's arrival. He is a capital fellow, vigorous, healthy, with no nerves, and even less imagination; and he has £2,000 a year into the bargain.

Periodically he makes me offers—the last was to travel round the world with him as secretary, which was a delicate way of paying my expenses and giving me some pocket-money—offers, however, which I invariably decline. I prefer to keep his friendship. Women could not come between us; money might—therefore I give it no opportunity. Chapter always laughed at what he called my "fancies", being himself possessed only of that thin-blooded quality of imagination which is ever associated with the prosaic-minded man. Yet, if taunted with this obvious lack, his wrath is deeply stirred. His psychology is that of the crass materialist—always a rather funny article. It will afford me genuine relief, none the less, to hear the cold judgment his mind will have to pass upon the story of this house as I shall have it to tell.

Dec. 2.—The strangest part of it all I have not referred to in this brief diary. Truth to tell, I have been afraid to set it down in black and white. I have kept it in the background of my thoughts, preventing it as far as possible from taking shape. In spite of my efforts, however, it has continued to grow stronger.

Now that I come to face the issue squarely it is harder to express than I imagined. Like a half-remembered melody that trips in the head but vanishes the moment you try to sing it, these thoughts form a group in the background of my mnind, behind my mind, as it were, and refuse to come forward. They are crouching ready to spring, but the actual leap

The Listener

never takes place.

In these rooms, except when my mind is strongly concentrated on my own work, I find myself suddenly dealing in thoughts and ideas that are not my own! New, strange conceptions, wholly foreign to my temperament, are for ever cropping up in my head. What precisely they are is of no particular importance. The point is that they are entirely apart from the channel in which my thoughts have hitherto been accustomed to flow. Especially they come when my mind is at rest, unoccupied; when I'm dreaming over the fire, or sitting with a book which fails to hold my attention. Then these thoughts which are not mine spring into life and make me feel exceedingly uncomfortable. Sometimes they are so strong that I almost feel as if someone were in the room beside me, thinking aloud.

Evidently my nerves and liver are shockingly out of order. I must work harder and take more vigorous exercise. The horrid thoughts never come when my mind is much occupied. But they are always there—waiting and as it were alive.

What I have attempted to describe above came first upon me gradually after I had been some days in the house, and then grew steadily in strength. The other strange thing has come to me.only twice in all these weeks. It appals me. It is the consciousness of the propinquity of some deadly and loathsome disease. It comes over me like a wave of fever heat, and then passes off, leaving me cold and trembling. The air seems for a few seconds to become tainted. So penetrating and convincing is the thought of this sickness, that on both occasions my brain has turned momentarily dizzy, and through my mind, like flames of white heat, have flashed the ominous names of all the dangerous illnesses I know. I can no more explain these visitations than I can fly, yet I know there is no dreaming about the clammy skin and palpitating heart which they always leave as witnesses of their brief visit.

Most strongly of all was I aware of this nearness of a mortal sickness when, on the night of the 28th, I went upstairs in pursuit of the listening figure. When we were shut in together in that little square room under the roof, I felt that I was face to face with the actual essence of this invisible and malignant disease. Such a feeling never entered my heart before, and I pray to God it never may again.

The Listener

There! Now I have confessed. I have given some expression at least to the feelings that so far I have been afraid to see in my own writing. For—since I can no longer deceive myself—the experiences of that night (28th) were no more a dream than my daily breakfast is a dream; and the trivial entry in this diary by which I sought to explain away an occurrence that caused me unutterable horror was due solely to my desire not to acknowledge in words what I really felt and believed to be true. The increase that would have accrued to my horror by so doing might have been more than I could stand.

Dec. 3.—I wish Chapter would come. My facts are all ready marshalled, and I can see his cool, grey eyes fixed incredulously on my face as I relate them: the knocking at my door, the well-dressed caller, the light in the upper window and the shadow upon the blind, the man who preceded me in the snow, the scattering of my clothes at night, Emily's arrested confession, the landlady's suspicious reticence, the midnight listener on the stairs, and those awful subsequent words in my sleep; and above all, and hardest to tell, the presence of the abominable sickness, and the stream of thoughts and ideas that are not my own.

I can see Chapter's face, and I can almost hear his deliberate words, "You've been at the tea again, and underfeeding, I expect, as usual. Better see my nerve doctor, and then come with me to the south of France." For this fellow, who knows nothing of disordered liver or high-strung nerves, goes regularly to a great nerve specialist with the periodical belief that his nervous system is beginning to decay.

Dec. 5.—Ever since the incident of the Listener, I have kept a night-light burning in my bedroom, and my sleep has been undisturbed. Last night, however, I was subjected to a far worse annoyance. I woke suddenly, and saw a man in front of the dressing-table regarding himself in the mirror. The door was locked, as usual. I knew at once it was the Listener, and the blood turned to ice in my veins. Such a wave of horror and dread swept over me that it seemed to turn me rigid in the bed, and I could neither move nor speak. I noted, however, that the odour I so abhorred was strong in the room.

The man seemed to be tall and broad. He was stooping forward over the mirror. His back was turned to me, but in the glass I saw the reflection of a huge head and face illumined fitfully by the flicker of the night-light. The spectral grey of very early morning stealing in round the edges of the curtains lent an additional horror to the picture, for it fell upon hair that was tawny and mane-like, hanging loosely about a face whose swollen, rugose features bore the once seen never forgotten leonine expression of— I dare not write down

The Listener

that awful word. But, byway of cor-roborative proof, I saw in the faint mingling of the two lights that there were several bronze-coloured blotches on the cheeks which the man was evidently examining with great care in the glass. The lips were pale and very thick and large. One hand I could not see, but the other rested on the ivory back of my hair-brush. Its muscles were strangely contracted, the fingers thin to emaciation, the back of the hand closely puckered up. It was like a big grey spider crouching to spring, or the claw of a great bird.

The full realisation that I was alone in the room with this nameless creature, almost within arm's reach of him, overcame me to such a degree that, when he suddenly turned and regarded me with small beady eyes, wholly out of proportion to the grandeur of their massive setting, I sat bolt upright in bed, uttered a loud cry, and then fell back in a dead swoon of terror upon the bed.

Dec. 5.—. . . When I came to this morning, the first thing I noticed was that my clothes were strewn all over the floor. . . . I find it difficult to put my thoughts together, and have sudden accesses of violent trembling. I determined that I would go at once to Chapter's hotel and find out when he is expected. I cannot refer to what happened in the night; it is too awful, and I have to keep my thoughts rigorously away from it. I feel light-headed and queer, couldn't eat any breakfast, and have twice vomited with blood. While dressing to go out, a hansom rattled up noisily over the cobbles, and a minute later the door opened, and to my great joy in walked the very subject of my thoughts.

The sight of his strong face and quiet eyes had an immediate effect upon me, and I grew calmer again. His very handshake was a sort of tonic. But, as I listened eagerly to the deep tones of his reassuring voice, and the visions of the night-time paled a little, I began to realise how very hard it was going to be to tell him my wild intangible tale. Some men radiate an animal vigour that destroys the delicate woof of a vision and effectually prevents its reconstruction.

Chapter was one of these men.

We talked of incidents that had filled the interval since we last met, and he told me something of his travels. He talked and I listened. But, so full was I of the horrid thing I had to tell, that I made a poor listener. I was for ever watching my opportunity to leap in and explode it all under his nose.

The Listener

Before very long, however, it was borne in upon me that he too was merely talking for time.

He too held something of importance in the background of his mind, something too weighty to let fall till the right moment presented itself. So that during the whole of the first half-hour we were both waiting for the psychological moment in which properly to release our respective bombs; and the intensity of our minds' action set up opposing forces that merely sufficed to hold one another in check—and nothing more. As soon as I realised this, therefore, I resolved to yield.

I renounced for the time my purpose of telling my story, and had the satisfaction of seeing that his mind, released from the restraint of my own, at once began to make preparations for the dis-charge of its momentous burden. The talk grew less and less magnetic; the interest waned; the descriptions of his travels became less alive. There were pauses between his sentences. Presently he repeated himself. His words clothed no living thoughts. The pauses grew longer. Then the interest dwindled altogether and went out like a candle in the wind. His voice ceased, and he looked up squarely into my face with serious and anxious eyes.

The psychological moment had come at last!

"I say—" he began, and then stopped short.

I made an unconscious gesture of encouragement, but said no word. I dreaded the impending.disclosure exceedingly. A dark shadow seemed to precede it.

"I say," he blurted out at last, "what in the world made you ever come to this place—to these rooms, I mean?"

"They're cheap, for one thing," I began, "and central and—"

"They're too cheap," he interrupted. "Didn't you ask what made 'em so cheap?"

"It never occurred to me at the time."

There was a pause in which he avoided my eyes.

The Listener

"For God's sake, go on, man, and tell it!" I cried, for the suspense was getting more than I could stand in my nervous condition.

"This was where Blount lived so long," he said quietly, "and where he—died. You know, in the old days I often used to come here and see him, and do what I could to alleviate his—" He stuck fast again.

"Well!" I said with a great effort. "Please go on— faster."

"But," Chapter went on, turning his face to the window with a perceptible shiver, "he finally got so terrible I simply couldn't stand it, though I always thought I could stand anything. It got on my nerves and made me dream, and haunted me day and night."

I stared at him, and said nothing. I had never heard of Blount in my life, and didn't know what he was talking about. But, all the same, I was trembling, and my mouth had become strangely dry.

"This is the first time I've been back here since," he said almost in a whisper, "and, 'pon my word, it gives me the creeps. I swear it isn't fit for a man to live in. I never saw you look so bad, old man."

"I've got it for a year," I jerked out, with a forced laugh; "signed the lease and all. I thought it was rather a bargain."

Chapter shuddered, and buttoned his overcoat up to his neck. Then he spoke in a low voice, looking occasionally behind him as though he thought someone was listening. I too could have sworn someone else was in the room with us.

"He did it himself, you know, and no one blamed him a bit; his sufferings were awful. For the last two years he used to wear a veil when he went out, and even then it was always in a closed carriage. Even the attendant who had nursed him for so long was at length obliged to leave. The extremities of both the lower limbs were gone, dropped off, and he moved about the ground on all fours with a sort of crawling motion. The odour, too, was——"

The Listener

I was obliged to interrupt him here. I could hear no more details of that sort. My skin was moist, I felt hot and cold by turns, for at last I was beginning to understand.

"Poor devil," Chapter went on; "I used to keep my eyes closed as much as possible. He always begged to be allowed to take his veil off, and asked if I minded very much. I used to stand by the open window. He never touched me, though. He rented the whole house. Nothing would induce him to leave it."

"Did he occupy—these very rooms?"

"No. He had the little room on the top floor, the square one just under the roof. He preferred it because it was dark. These rooms were too near the ground, and he was afraid people might see him through the windows. A crowd had been known to follow him up to the very door, and then stand below the windows in the hope of catching a glimpse of his face."

"But there were hospitals."

"He wouldn't go near one, and they didn't like to force him. You know, they say it's not contagious, so there was nothing to prevent his staying here if he wanted to. He spent all his time.reading medical books, about drugs and so on. His head and face were something appalling, just like a lion's."

I held up my hand to arrest further description.

"He was a burden to the world, and he knew it. One night I suppose he realised it too keenly to wish to live. He had the free use of drugs—and in the morning he was found dead on the floor.

Two years ago, that was, and they said then he had still several years to live."

"Then, in Heaven's name!" I cried, unable to bear the suspense any longer, "tell me what it was he had, and be quick about it."

"I thought you knew!" he exclaimed, with genuine surprise. "I thought you knew!"

The Listener

He leaned forward and our eyes met. In a scarcely audible whisper I caught the words his lips seemed almost afraid to utter:

"He was a leper!"

CPSIA information can be obtained
at www.ICGtesting.com
Printed in the USA
LVHW060427250321
682419LV00023B/237